WORKSONG

WORKSONG

WRITTEN BY

Gary Paulsen

ILLUSTRATED BY

Ruth Wright Paulsen

Voyager Books
Harcourt, Inc.
SAN DIEGO   NEW YORK   LONDON

Requests for permission to make copies of any part of the work should be
 mailed to the following address: Permissions Department, Harcourt, Inc.,
6277 Sea Harbor Drive, Orlando, Florida 32887-6777.

First Voyager Books edition 2000
Voyager Books is a registered trademark of Harcourt, Inc.

The Library of Congress has cataloged the hardcover edition as follows:
Paulsen, Gary.
Worksong/written by Gary Paulsen; illustrated by Ruth Wright Paulsen.
p.   cm.
Summary: Illustrations and rhyming text depict people doing all kinds of work.
[1. Occupations—Fiction.   2. Stories in rhyme.] I. Paulsen, Ruth Wright, ill.   II. Title.
PZ8.3.27369Wo   1997
[E]—dc20   95-49309
ISBN 0-15-200980-9
ISBN 0-15-202371-2 pb

L K J I

Printed in Singapore

*This book is dedicated
with all admiration and respect
to Nancy Flannery*

It is keening noise and jolting sights,

and hammers flashing in the light,

and houses up and
trees in sun,

and trucks on one more nighttime run.

It is fresh new food to fill the plates,

and flat, clean sidewalks to try to skate,
and towering buildings that were not there,
hanging suddenly in the air.

It is offices filled with
glowing screens

and workers making steel beams,

and ice-cream cones to lick and wear,

and all the pins that
hold your hair.

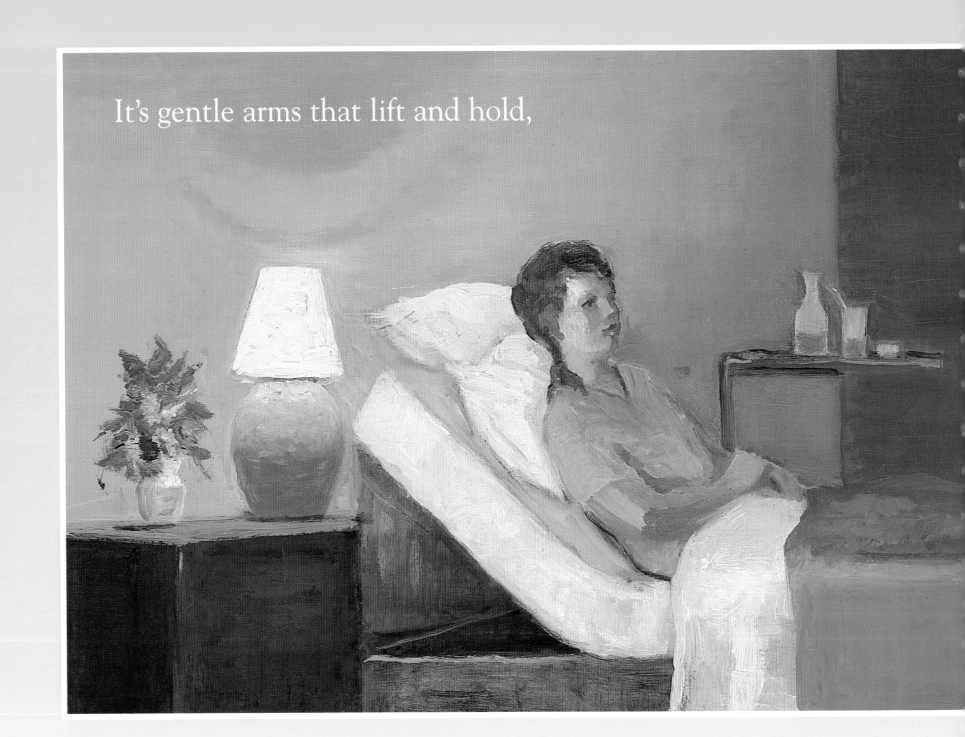

It's gentle arms that lift and hold,

and all the soldiers
brave and bold,

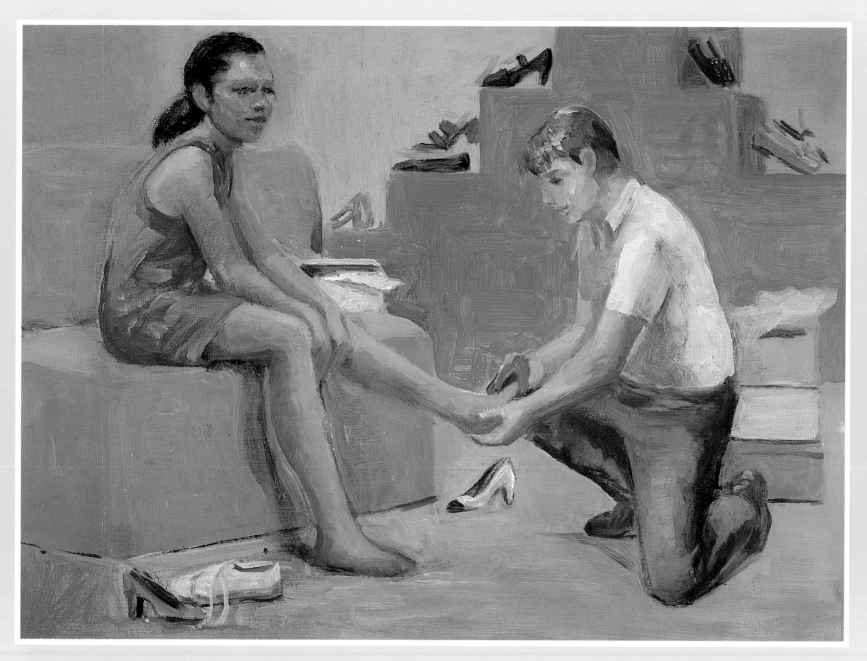

and help to fit the brand-new shoes,

and hands to show you books to use.

It is people here and
people there, making
things for all to share;

all the things there are to be,
and nearly all there is to see.

And when the day is paid and done,

and all the errands
have been run,

it's mother, father in a chair,
with tired eyes and loosened hair.

Resting short but
loving long,

resting for the next day's song.

The illustrations in this book were done in oils on canvas.

The display type was set in Colwell.

The text type was set in Goudy.

Color separations by Bright Arts, Ltd., Singapore

Printed and bound by Tien Wah Press, Singapore

Production supervision by Stanley Redfern and Pascha Gerlinger

Designer by Michael Farmer